I0726298

Formula-12

Bryan Nowak

This is a work of fiction.

Names, characters, businesses, places, events, or incidents are either the products of the author's imagination or used in a fictitious manner. Any resemblance to actual person, living or dead, or actual events is purely coincidental.

Formula-12

copyright © 2022 Bryan Nowak

All rights reserved.
Published by DreamPunk Press
Cover design by: Bryan Nowak and portfolio.mo
(http://www.portfolimo.com/)

DreamPunk Press uses OpenDyslexic font from
www.opendyslexic.org

978-1-954214-28-6 Open Dyslexic
978-1-954214-29-3 Déjà vu
978-1-954214-30-9 e-Pub

The U.S. Army Surgeon General's Medical Research and Development Board

Report #563271: Transcript of Interview with Dr. Ulf Schmitz

Recorded: 17 May 1946

Location: Fort Deitrich, Maryland

Interviewer: Dr. Stephen Kozlowski, COL U.S. Army

Subject: Dr. Ulf Schmitz

Former Position: Professor of Viral Biology and Epidemiology

Military Rank (if applicable): Colonel; Medical Corps

Prisoner Number: 247569-17B

/////////BEGINNING OF TRANSCRIPT/////////

Interviewer: The time is 0838, 17 May 1946. My name is Dr. Kozlowski and I am interviewing the German doctor, and prisoner, Ulf Schmitz, about the events which took place in Germany during the war and his part in those events. Dr., if you would please, begin at the beginning.

Dr. Schmitz: Naturally, it would be impractical for me to begin in the middle of the story and it would be unlikely to have any scientific value. And yet, as I told the first interviewer, I will retell the story to anyone who will listen. It is an important one.

You must understand the situation is difficult for me to recount. So much has happened in such a short amount of time. All the things I have seen. All the things I did, that I had to do, which went against what I truly believe as a scientist.

I know what you think of me, but I'm just as human as the next man. I lost a lot of good friends and colleagues. Reliving their deaths is difficult for me. But, I will go over it again if you wish, so we can put this business behind us once and for all. And maybe some good can come of an unspeakable horror.

I was working at my laboratory at the airbase. I am pretty sure it was a Wednesday, but I can't be sure anymore. Anyway, we were working—

Interviewer: Forgive me Doctor Schmitz, but where exactly was this?

Dr. Schmitz: Yes, of course. Rangsdorf Airfield, just south of Berlin. But the location is not as important as it might seem. We were in fairly non-descript buildings. Anyway, it was an unseasonably warm summer. It was August of 1943, I forget the exact day and I am not sure it has any special significance.

Anyway, as I was saying, I was working with several examples of the bioweapon I was sure would give the Third Reich the very thing it needed to ensure victory over the allies.

I see now I was arrogant and will pay for my crimes, perhaps at the end of an executioner's rope. I suppose it is better to say that I shall burn in hell for the crimes I committed. Here on earth, I shall be condemned to work on this Frankenstein's monster I have created for many years to come. But perhaps I have become a little wiser.

I was working at my test tubes in the laboratory at the end of the airfield when a noise roused me from my careful measurements. I turned and saw my old friend, and close colleague, Colonel Erik Hauptmann enter the room with his usual large smile. He said, "Greetings, Herr Doctor Schmitz. I bring all the best salutations from Berlin."

He had a smile that could brighten the sun itself. A welcome sight to see after spending too much time in my cramped laboratory. Not that it mattered, but he was a large man, being of Northern Prussian ancestry of the purest kind. Striking man really.

I inquired of him if he had a good trip from Juvincourt Airfield in occupied France. You understand, made small talk, as you Americans say, as I went about finishing up my experiment. I knew the real reason for his visit was that I had promised results. Fortunately, I had something positive to report.

As I am sure you are aware now, official reports of German successes on the battlefield were infused with fabrication and the officers, of which I was a commissioned Colonel, knew the reality. At that time, we understood the war would be lost if we didn't find a new weapon soon. This was my task.

A bioweapon to end all question of who is the dominant power on Earth. Did you ever think what would happen if a gas could be spread on the field of battle which not only would, ultimately, kill intended victims but throw them into a rage. Turn them into killing machines willing to rip their comrades limb from limb? Ach, ja. A great leap forward in warfare.

Don't look at me with such contempt gentlemen. I know how it sounds. I caution you to stay your judgement. I am a bioweapons scientist, not a madman. If you don't think the Soviets are doing the same, you are either a fool or insane.

Interviewer: We wouldn't insinuate such a thing, Doctor, or we wouldn't be having this conversation while other members of your party are occupying a cell in Nuremburg. Please, continue.

Dr. Schmitz: Well, anyway, I continued my small talk with Erik as I worked. He was here to witness my greatest triumph to date. The next experiment was a practical test of my latest formula. And I was optimistic. We were so close to making it work. I had it fine-tuned to work on primates, and I ushered Erik over to the viewing area.

I said, "You see, Erik, in these cages we have three monkeys." I motioned to my assistant, Fräulein Weber, to initiate the trial. She naturally did exactly as instructed and prepared to lower the glass patrician between where we were standing and the caged animals.

I took out a syringe from the drawer and drew in a measured amount of my latest formula, F-12, as I numbered the formulas. Erik looked on and asked, "Ulf, does the formula pose a threat to us, standing here?"

"No, it doesn't. Until it mixes with blood, it will not be fully activated. Then you will see what it can do." I placed the syringe in the end of a specially developed stick allowing me to inject the rhesus monkeys without danger to myself. They are a little like children who avoid needles if they can.

I pointed the stick at the nearest monkey and gave him a quick jab. People might think that it is hard to inject a small monkey, but it is surprising simple when you get used to it. And I have had a lot of practice over the years. Next, we would move from monkeys to maybe a few prisoners and finally on a few volunteers who are at the peak of physical prowess. Naturally they will have no idea what they are signing up for. We really don't want to—

Interviewer: I get the point, Doctor, you can continue.

Dr. Schmitz: Quite right. After the injection, I pulled the stick out of the cage and Fräulein Weber lowered the glass shield in place and we watched. F-12 takes a few moments to mutate, but only a few moments. It works fast, as I designed it to. The replication process of the biological agent is so quick that once someone is infected, it will take moments, as my friend Erik observed.

The monkey, which had calmed down moments after the injection began to sway back and forth on its legs. The unfortunate primate shivered and pulled at its fur uncontrollably. Really, it is terrifying to watch. But as a scientist, fascinating, as well. Pieces of fur were falling out of its skin at an alarming rate. The other two animals pushed their way to the back of the cage, the only place they knew had a door that could offer escape.

There was simply no escape. Which was really the point of it all.

Erik stepped away from the cages and gave Fräulein Weber a dubious glance. She only smiled, as she knew what to expect. Thinking back on it now, it is surprising to me that a woman could be almost sociopathic in her approach to what we were doing there. Alas, such is the way with bioweapons technicians, I suppose. Not work for the faint of heart.

I tell you the ferocity of this animal was alarming. The test subject leapt on the nearest of its cell mates and began ripping and tearing at it. Eventually, the infected monkey began bashing its fellow roommate's head into the wall of the cage until it was dead. Next, it turned toward the remaining creature and went on the attack. Midway through its second attempted murder, the test monkey just stopped what it was doing, closed its eyes, and fell dead to the bottom of the cage. Blood gushed from its nose, as it had in every iteration of the test that I ran.

Erik was so happy, he was almost giddy, I tell you. I had to quiet his enthusiasm, though. This was a successful test on a lower primate. We still needed to retry the test again and once we were sure of the result, start working our way up from there.

Erik finally took control of himself and said, "Ulf, I have never witnessed anything so terrifying in my life." He took a few steps forward and examined the blood, bile, hair, and tissue that now painted the inner side of the glass.

Our minor celebration was interrupted by the door opening in the back of the room. A young German soldier entered the room carrying a large box. I thanked the young man for bringing me the parcel I was anxiously waiting on. Part of another experiment, it was the latest shipment of the new gas masks.

"Erik, you may want to take a look at these."

"What do we have here? A new gas mask?" He held it up to the light and frowned at it before remarking, "There is no hose to connect it to anything."

"My dear, Colonel, there are no hoses. These are the latest and greatest in gas defense for the modern battlefield." I reached into the box and pulled out a small cylinder wrapped in wax paper. I screwed it into the side of the mask and placed the cord around my neck to hold it in place. I demonstrated the thing for him.

NOTE: SUBJECT STOPPED TALKING FOR A FEW MINUTES

Interviewer: Doctor, I am sorry to interrupt. You were telling us about the gas mask.

Dr. Schmitz: I apologize, of course. I was just thinking that if I could go back to that moment in time, I could have saved my friend. Regrets are the heaviest things to carry around with you in life.

That very same mask I placed around my neck sits there on the desk. Had I not done that, there is a good chance I wouldn't be here right now to share with you this tale.

Erik was thrilled with the progress. He told me that there would be a commendation in my work on the masks. Hoses were a consistent nuisance on the battlefield and our work represented a leap forward. German soldiers were now truly the most advanced in the world.

Erik had only stopped in for a quick look at what I was working on before he needed to go back to Berlin and check in with Reich's Minister, Herr Rust and der Führer himself. I was certain that his report would buy me a little more time to complete my work and truly develop a bioweapon that could change the tide of the war.

My friend, being so large, was also clumsy. Turning toward the door, you see, his massive wool coat swept out behind him and caught the corner of the shelf that had contained many different samples I was working with. The clothing caught the corner of the shelf and brought the whole thing down, crashing to the floor, pinning poor Fräulein Weber to the floor. The vials containing my latest solutions, awaiting testing, spilled out on the floor.

The unfortunate fräulein, who we can rightly call the mother of all zombies, sliced her hands, arms, and legs on the glass spread all over the floor.

You will remember, gentlemen, that I said the bioweapon needs blood to activate. Well, it did just that and it was alarming how quickly it took over her smaller frame. Another one of those heavy regrets I'll carry around for the rest of my life.

Naturally, Erik yelled over her screams, "Oh mein Gott, Fräulein, I'm so sorry!" He grabbed a few towels from the table while simultaneously lifting the shelf from the stricken girl. But what happened next, I wasn't even prepared for, and will never forget it as long as I live.

You know, gentlemen, it is funny to me in an ironic sort of way, how often we say we will never forget an event as long as we live and never really mean it. But I can tell you this is burned into my soul. To know that I orchestrated this series of events down to the last DNA sequence haunts me day and night.

The unfortunate girl, pretty young thing, and smart, too, stopped thrashing and I could see a change come over her. Like my test subjects, her skin went ashen and the major veins in her face took on a black hue. For the briefest of moments, she stopped moving.

I tried to warn Erik to back away from her. There was nothing he could do to save her and as a matter of recourse, I ordered everyone out of the laboratory. For I could see the F-12 taking over her body and mind, as assuredly as I could see a cup of water change color after a tea bag had been steeping in it. F-12 works far faster than tea.

Sadly, for my friend Erik, it was too late. His compassion for others and his defiance in the face of his own peril overrode his common sense. Had he heeded my warning, we may have been all right. It was possible that we could have prevented what was to come next and the reason I sit before you now.

Erik glanced away from the stricken girl, only a fraction of a second, but it was enough. She was reanimated into something more insidious than anything before. My former assistant grabbed my friend's arm with a quickness and power that I would have considered impossible had I not known what F-12 was capable of.

She bit into the fleshy part of his hand. You know, the side with the thumb. He screamed and she pulled him in closer and took a bite out of his neck. He was powerless to stop her and, very likely, she was powerless to stop herself. Blood flew everywhere in the room. It was all I could do to push myself away from the scene and run toward the door.

Naturally, I scanned the room to make sure the last of my assistants had left and then I exited the door myself. Quickly, I barred the door after me, so no one could get out. I watched through the window as Erik went through a similar process as the young Fräulein Weber.

Interviewer: Describe to me what you saw happen to your friend.

Dr. Schmitz: It was the same as before. Skin ashen, blood vessels turn a sickly dark color. Animalistic instincts taking over and higher reasoning being erased. He and Fräulein Weber, now both reduced to their primordial selves, attacked the door ferociously. Thankfully bioweapons labs are built of stronger stuff, and they were contained.

I am not ashamed to admit that while my mother was intensely religious, I am not. However, in that moment, I prayed to Gott to deliver me from this situation. I just sort of stood there, watching them through the window, trying to understand the ramifications of what had just happened. Both of them were dead, at least on the rational level. Replaced by an automaton's understanding nothing but violence.

Interviewer: Wait a minute, Doctor, I thought you told us that the formula was designed to kill its host.

Dr. Schmitz: True. However, in human subjects, I found it takes a significantly longer time for the formulation to come to its natural conclusion. Instead of minutes, as in the rhesus monkey, humans can go on like that for months, I suspected at the time.

And yet, my focus on my friend and former colleague was only momentary. You see, my attention was taken in a different direction. The flames and smoke overtaking the room.

Interviewer: Sorry for the additional interruption, but I would have thought a fire would be the best of all outcomes. Are you suggesting that was not the case?

Dr. Schmitz: Forgive me, I do not boast, but my intelligence quotient is quite a bit higher than most people. I consider you both to be of above average intelligence, but my mind works on the formulas of my creation and the addition of many other variables so quickly I can see things that most people would be incapable of comprehending.

That smoke meant something else entirely different to me. I considered thousands of possible permutations the addition of the smoke might mean. Sadly, about sixty percent of those permutations led me to the conclusion that any particulate matter created by the smoke would likely be just as deadly as a bite from the creatures I had created.

Interviewer: You mean F-12 created.

Dr. Schmitz: You can try and make the situation look better than it does if you would like, but I accept what happened. Blood is on my hands, and I must learn to accept that. Let me continue, please.

Smoke pushed its way from under the eaves of my small laboratory building. Knowing what I know about my own creation, I pushed my assistants farther away from the structure. I wanted them clear of the smoke. I sent a few of them back to the barracks building, which I knew was not only far away from the fire, but upwind. They would be safe there, or so I thought.

I need you to understand that I tried to stop them. I begged and pleaded, but they would not listen. They only brushed me aside. They were running to their deaths, and I could do nothing to stop them. Nothing more than kids, they were younger soldaten. Children really. And I could not—

Interviewer: Who are you talking about?

Dr. Schmitz: Sorry, it is hard for me to recollect this. A group of well-meaning soldiers. These were young enlistees from local families, two sergeants, and a major, posted to provide security for the airbase. They moved forward with buckets of fire retardant, trying to put out the blaze. Smoke and ash took to the sky. A fire devil rose through the center of the building. It looked like Satan himself staring down at us.

One of the soldiers, a corporal I think, dropped his bucket and started clawing at his face.

His fingernails scratched away skin and left rivers of blood streaming down his face. The other soldiers, not noticing, went on with their work. They were unaware of their colleague until he attacked them with his bare hands, biting at them and scratching at the others, just like the monkeys in the cage.

It was then that I knew my hypothesis was correct. The smoke was just as bad as the injection itself. I needed to do something to stop it, but what? Well, I felt a strange tug around my neck and realized I still had the mask around my neck. So, I put it on, realizing it was the only thing likely to keep me from succumbing to the horror unfolding around me.

I screamed at them, "Get away from the building, all of you!" There was little I could do. F-12 moved far quicker than even I could have predicted. After the second and third soldiers were attacked, they, too, were infected by the biological agent.

Interviewer: How is that even possible, Doctor? I can't think of any contagion that works that fast.

Dr. Schmitz: Because I engineered it to work that way. To spread with alarming efficiency, it jumps from host to host through the smoke, as well as the bites from other soldiers.

One of the soldiers had dropped his gear on the ground before he launched into fighting that fateful blaze. There was a bayonet. I took it and ran toward the blaze. I wanted to try and put the ones who were infected out of their turmoil as fast as possible.

To my astonishment, a few had already run off into the woods surrounding the building. There was little I could do to bring them back. All I could do was kill the ones nearest to me and hope to find the others, or that maybe people would realize the danger and take actions on their own, but there was no way to be sure.

The soldier who had brought in the gas masks was standing there. I grabbed him by the shoulders with hopes he might be able to be saved.

The boy turned to me and stared. I tell you, his eyes were dead. Skin just as pale as that of a porcelain doll. He still wore his uniform and his stahlhelm on his head, making him look like the perfect German soldier. And yet, he could no longer even be considered human anymore.

I want to say his name was Meyer. But that's not important. He hit me with unbelievable strength. Such strength you can't even imagine. I was lifted off the ground. I lost the bayonet while tumbling across the ground. Meyer was on me in and instant.

The young lads face was contorted in a vicious sneer. He snapped at me like a wild dog. In all my life I had never seen anything like that. It was both amazing and incredible. That a human being could be taken from a perfectly normal and rational state, even a German soldier, and turned into a monster willing to tear apart another human was unbelievable. I knew the bioweapon would work, but I did not know—

Interviewer: Doctor, I am sorry, but can we please get on with the story.

Dr. Schmitz: Sorry, yes. It was just so amazing seeing the weapon work. Even more impressive to feel the raw power I had unleased.

Well, as you can imagine, I struggled to get back to the bayonet while simultaneously fighting off Meyer, who was trying to rip and tear into my flesh. I say again, you cannot imagine how strong these, I suppose you would call them zombies, are. It is unbelievable how hard I had to fight. But I knew if I gave in just an inch, I would be lost.

And it was then that I suppose I began to consider how, if I lost, it could also mean so was Germany. If this contagion made it outside of the base, it would be nothing to have it take over Europe with a ferocity that would make the plague look like a mere child's game.

Meyer continued to take swipes at me, and worst of all, he was focusing on my mask. I knew time was quickly running out. I pride myself in being in good physical shape, but exhaustion was setting in.

That was when I noticed the Luger in Meyer's belt. I orchestrated a move where I could push Meyer to the left while reaching down with my right. I grabbed the pistol and shoved the weapon into Meyer's chin and fired two shots.

The former German soldier went slack at my side. I stared at him for a moment before the sounds of the walls collapsing behind me shook me from my momentary state of shock. There was more that had to be done.

I rummaged through Meyer's pockets and pulled out two magazines for the Luger. Out of the corner of my eye, toward the tree line, I saw movement and turned to face the Major who had had come to fight the fire. He too had succumbed to the bioweapon.

Interviewer: How could you tell before you pulled the trigger? Didn't you check?

Dr. Schmitz: Natürlich, I checked. Skin and veins were the same as the others. I made a quick decision and put a round into his head, sending the Major reeling backwards to the ground.

There was little else I could do. I could already hear a fire engine screaming toward the facility, but they would be far too late to really do anything other than seal their own doom. I needed to get back to my office on the administrative side of the base if I were to have any chance of saving any of these people. My notes and some samples were in my office. The antidote was a simple matter, and I could easily make it and administer it to those infected, provided the numbers remained low enough.

To my left, the Major's kubelwagon remained with its engine idling. I ran to the vehicle and jumped over the door, sliding into the driver's seat. I got rolling and hit the throttle the exact moment another victim of F-12 stumbled out of the woods. With no other choice, I drove over the undead soldier, sending blood and a helmet still containing the head of the unfortunate victim flying over the top of the vehicle.

I glanced up, only for a moment at the helmet to see the dead eyes of the unfortunate victim imploring me to do something to stop the madness. His mouth was slightly open in a partial scream of what I would come to understand was the scream of the undead I had created.

Interviewer: An unnecessary detail, Doctor.

Dr. Schmitz: Oh, my dear man, do not get squeamish on me. We are only really getting started, mein Freund. As it turned out, things were going to get far worse before we had any real hope of anything improving for anyone. You have no concept of the lives lost and the lies told afterward to cover up the horrors and, dare I say, atrocities. They all have their root cause in one man and that man is sitting here, telling you his tale.

Where was I? Oh yes, no longer worrying about roads, I cut through a small stand of trees and entered onto the airfield. The scene was utter chaos. I could hear several soldiers, nearer to the barracks, seemingly alarmed by the commotion, firing at an alarmingly ferocious enemy. At the same time, people they knew. Friends even. The exponential nature of the growing tidal wave of zombies was too much. It was far worse than I had even anticipated. There was little they could do to hold their position, no matter how much ammunition they had.

Interviewer: Why's that?

Dr. Schmitz: F-12 acts in the brain and nervous system and is designed to continue under all circumstances, until every nerve is completely under its control and then it eventually kills the victim. Although this mutation seemed to allow the victim to live considerably longer than in the rhesus monkeys. However, there is one thing that will stop the reaction.

As you no doubt already understand, a direct shot to the brainstem or completely severing the head. That is where the biological element will continue to function until such a time as it is ordered to end the life of its host. However, if that junction between brain and body is severed, that would mean the end of the whole reaction itself.

For purposes of my retelling, it is important to understand that the airfield was an old Prussian airfield used in the first world war. A wall, a meter thick, separated the airfield from the rest of the base, with the exception of a thick metal gate that is closed most of the time. If that entry is closed, the airfield has no way in and no way out.

Although I had no evidence, or maybe it was wishful thinking on my part, I theorized the victims, in their ambling state would likely lack the muscle coordination to climb over a high barrier. While engineering F-12, I suppressed fine motor skills and increased the gross motor functions.

Interviewer: Strong but not very nimble?

Dr. Schmitz: Precisely. So, I crossed the airfield in the car. I had to swerve out of the way of a Bücker aircraft on final approach to the landing strip. I tried to wave the pilot off, but it is unlikely he could see me while landing.

Eight undead pushed their way onto the airfield from a small barracks in the woods that was used for transient military personnel who were temporarily assigned to the base. The unfortunate pilot, not realizing the situation, brought the plane to a stop in front of a hangar not too far from the creatures that he probably thought were the groundcrew. The gaggle of zombies reached the plane and pulled the pilot out from his seat through a hole they tore in the fabric of the aircraft.

The pilot screamed and shrieked as the zombies yanked the man through mechanical instrumentation, cables, and aircraft frame. It was carnage of the kind that I had never seen before. If you never have, I certainly hope you never witness another human being ripped to shreds. I was powerless to help the aviator. And yet, I was still thankful the unfortunate man in the Bücker slowed the progression of zombies. A terrible thing to think, to be sure, but I was taking my blessings where I could get them.

I could see the old Prussian wall standing sentinel. And from what I could tell, the steel door looked closed. A small, yet growing, group of undead scratched and shrieked to get into the complex but I knew the gates were built to hold back anything short of a tank attacking.

I wrenched the wheel to the left and put the car into skid, bringing me alongside the wall. I had a few hundred meters to go before slamming into the next wall, so I made sure to give myself space between the gate and where I thought I would have to stop.

Unfortunately for me, and probably fortunately for him, I saw an undead Schutzstaffel officer meandering in circles in front of me. I hit the brakes, but not in time to avoid pinning the unfortunate SS officer against the wall along with his hands and arms. The unfortunate thing growled and shrieked at me. For you know, that is what those things do, growl and shriek.

It was unfortunately stuck between me and where I needed to go. So, I did the only reasonable thing I could do in that situation, and I used his head as a step stool. With it I was able to jump to the top of the wall and hoist myself over. But before going, I took a moment to do the right thing and shoot the poor creature in the head, putting it out of its misery.

Interviewer: Not sure I would call an SS officer a poor creature.

Dr. Schmitz: My dear deluded friend, an SS officer is a thing we now view with ridicule and scorn. One turned into a zombie is no more capable of resisting its carnal urge to kill and feed on the living than you or I would be able to turn ourselves into ostriches or giraffes. They are just as worthy of being delivered from their turmoil as anyone else.

Interviewer: So, you made it over the wall, then what?

Dr. Schmitz: A series of events made me rethink every decision I had made in my entire life. In particular, those decisions made me reconsider the utility of my life's work. Reanimating the dead may have been something better left to the almighty than me, a humble scientist with an extraordinary gift.

Interview: How humble of you.

Dr. Schmitz: Indeed, I was starting to feel my place in the world and perhaps I had overstepped my boundaries.

Still, I cannot tell you how relieved I was to be on the other side of that wall. At least, for the moment, it felt like I could take a moment to breathe and think through my next actions.

The formulas for all the test vials I had made were in my office, where I kept copies of my work. It allowed me to think of them over a pipe and a snifter of brandy at night where my brain was not so encumbered by the rigors of the laboratory setting. Occasionally, I would invite colleagues over to talk over my work and play chess.

Fond memories, but I was not there to relax. I needed to make it to my office and gain copies of documents and samples. I ran toward the direction of the gate where I could access the walkway up to the main office building where my suite of rooms was.

As you can imagine, the crowd gathered at the noises from the airfield. I heard occasional gunshots from people presumably stuck and forced to face the growing menace. I shuddered to think of those poor people, but I really didn't have time to process all of it. I needed to make my way to the office to gain access to my laboratory notes and the few samples I kept in the safe.

Interviewer: Excuse me, Doctor, were the samples important?

Dr. Schmitz: Excellent question. Not really. The antidote was surprisingly simple to manufacture and could be aerosolized in no time at all. However, having a few samples with me would allow me to synthesize the antidote faster and continue my studies on what I had created. I had no time to reflect on how a simple Bestäubungsflugzeug, or crop-dusting plane as you

Americans call it, could suffice to distribute the chemicals.

However, synthesizing enough of the antidote was a problem. We had a laboratory at the facility that could make it in sufficient quantities, but I would need to hurry.

I shoved open the door to the office and went immediately to the safe. As I extracted my papers, something outside the building caught my attention. You see, my office overlooks the main gate and since it had been warm, the windows were open. I clearly heard the voices of two people arguing.

One of them I knew to be a soldier, a first sergeant by the name of Bremar. He was a senior sergeant and oversaw the security forces. A good chap, loyal to the cause, and followed most orders to the letter. It was his penchant for following orders that really caught my ear.

He was arguing with another man, who I unfortunately also knew. That man was Major Stern. Ironically, that means star in German. Which is what he was not. However, Major Stern believed himself to be only one or two ears away from Hitler himself. He was an arrogant ass who knew nothing and was capable of even less.

Stern was shouting at Bremar to open the gate. Bremar argued that given what they were seeing on the other side of the gate, they could not open it for risk to the other soldiers. He had watched first-hand what was happening and tried to make the Major understand. Of course, the Major was not capable of comprehending the proper use of a hat box let alone anything Bremar was saying.

This went on while I watched them from the window. I tried to shout down to them, but it seemed like the noise was too much for me to be heard. So, I grabbed what I needed from the safe and put them into my satchel. I turned to head downstairs to tell the Major he was being a horse's ass when a shot rang out.

Well naturally, I ducked for a moment as the shot sounded like it came from right under my window. Then I ventured out and saw what had happened; Stern had shot Bremar in the head and was now opening the gate himself.

You can imagine what I thought about it, and I started screaming as loud as I could. And yet, there was no way I could stop him. Added to that, the moment the gates opened, the unfortunate victims of F-12 poured through the opening like an ocean that had found a proverbial crack in the dike.

The screams were horrifying. Sometimes, those screams come back to me at night. And do you want to know what is really interesting? Only one of those men really sticks out in my head. There was a poor kid, no more than sixteen standing there. He looked almost silly in his Wehrmacht uniform. Like he was going to a costume ball dressed in his father's uniform.

Anyway, this poor boy had the look of abject terror on his face as he was overtaken by the zombies. He screamed for his mother. I heard him clearly over the noise. Unbelievable, I know. I did not have long to listen to his torment, as moments later he was torn to shreds by the undead creatures. I will never forget that face.

Images will haunt me for the rest of my life, but in the moment, I knew I had to get moving. Downstairs, the monsters of my creation poured through the door and into the building with an almost deafening racket. Muffled gunfire reverberated through the hallways or maybe my hearing was affected by the sounds of the shooting.

Glass doors, cabinets, and other things were smashed by the unholy beasts clawing their way over whatever the soldaten could throw in their paths. With their increased strength, and their appetite for the flesh of the living, there was little anyone could do to prevent them from pushing through any obstacles in their path.

To the left of my office door, away from the main stairwell, there was another stairwell that led to an outer door. The coast appeared clear, so I ran for it.

Interviewer: But, Doctor, I thought you said you were going to manufacture the cure there in your laboratory.

Dr. Schmitz: Ah, yes, I did and I fully intended to. Unfortunately for me, once the undead took over the first floor, there was nothing I could do as I was certain that many of the glasses being smashed were likely the instruments in my laboratory being rendered useless by the undead.

As I said, I made it to the bottom of the stairs without a problem. I looked out the door and into the parking area behind the building for anything amiss. I didn't see anything, however—

Oh wait, let me back up a moment, I suppose I should explain. You see, the building had a front and a back door that, if you entered the front door, you could immediately walk to the back door without stopping. Both main doors sat directly in the middle of the building. Stairways in the middle and at the extreme ends of the building would provide access to the parking lot. Since I was at the far end of the building, I reasoned that I should be able to make my escape from a growing German zombie army.

I glanced outside the door at the parking lot, which looked deserted. Most of the commotion in the front of the building cleared the parking lot of anyone who might be smoking cigarettes at the little gazebo behind the building.

As the zombies seemed perfectly content to amble through the building in search for victims, I carefully made my way into the parking lot. I tried to be as quiet as possible, to not attract the creatures. They appeared to be more interested in the noises inside, and as long as they were occupied in the building, I had little to worry about.

I began checking cars as I knew a few people left the keys for the cars under the overhead shade. I had to be very careful, you see, German cars were not what you would call robust at the time and the doors made a great deal of noise. Carefully, I moved from vehicle to vehicle and had a very hard time finding one with keys in it or one of the older ones that did not require keys.

To my left, a back gate that was normally open during the day, sat open to the world. The soldiers who normally guarded it were gone, likely attracted to the commotion inside the building. If I was able to find a vehicle, I could make it to the gate and, hopefully, lock the madness erupting inside the building away until I had a solution in hand.

To my surprise, a German staff car pulled into the driveway with an entourage of about four other cars.

Then I remembered that today was a visit from the head of the German Cryogenics Office, a General Gitner, I think his name was.

Of course, I tried to warn them to keep going, but there was nothing I could do as I was too far away from them to communicate the danger. Plus, I risked being heard by the hordes of murderous beings in the building if I made too much of a racket.

The front of the building, where the parking lot was, had a huge circle in front of it with a large fountain that reminded me of a Roman fountain or something you would see in Greece. It was left over from when the building was part of the Prussian Science Academy in the 1800s and featured a statue of the god Apollo.

As per most general officer's motorcades, this one had two cars in front of the staff car and two in the back. As you can imagine—

Interviewer: Herr Doctor, what does this have to do with the story?

Dr. Schmitz: That is the trouble with you Americans. No patience. Do you also read the pages out of the middle of a book before reading the first chapters? No,

I didn't think so. Please, let me continue and you will find out.

As I was saying, two in front, the staff car, and two in the back. The cars all stopped at about the same time with the staff car, naturally, directly in front of the door to the building. The general's aid jumped out of the front car and ran to the back to open the door for her boss.

Pretty thing, blonde hair, impossibly tall. Reminded me of one of those Viking women, Valkyries, I believe they are called. When she closed her car door, she slammed it and that would be their final undoing. The general stepped out of his car, straightened the jacket of his dress uniform, and turned toward the building.

His eyes raised to the door of the building just in time to see the glass, wood, and metal of the door give under the weight of a league of Nazi zombies alerted to their presence by the slamming of that car door. The look on his face, I am ashamed to admit, I found a little comical. There was a brief moment when he looked like something smashing through the door was the most natural thing in the world. Then his face changed to one of abject terror as the flood poured out onto the porch and down the stairs.

The beasts clawed and reached over one another, stumbling down the stairs like a sort of writhing waterfall of former humans. All their faces bore the same dark vein coloration I had seen with Hauptman and the others.

Instantly, the cars were emptied of fools trying to save the general.

Beg your pardon. I should not call them fools. They had no way of knowing.

But there was no time to think of that then. The zombies grabbed the general and made a meal of him. He was dead in an instant. They moved to the left side of the column of cars, killing and devouring enlisted and officers where they stood. I witnessed one poor feldwebel, I guess you might call him a staff sergeant in the American army, crawling toward the relative protection of one of the cars. He almost made it when one of his former colleagues grabbed him by the leg and took a large chunk out of his calf muscle. Blood spurted everywhere and the unfortunate soldaten screamed out in pain.

The pretty general's aid was the least fortunate of all, as her torment would continue for some time to come unless someone took pity on her. She managed to shake off a few of the monsters and climb to the top of the large fountain and scale the statue of Apollo.

This put her high enough that the writhing mass of animals were unable to get to her, but left her no way to escape. She could not get down and make a run for the car, as she would be immediately attacked, and I knew there was no way to save her life from my vantage point.

Interviewer: What did you do?

Dr. Schmitz: I did the only thing I could think of to do. I made a break for the car she had been in. Fortunately, the zombies were so entranced with her, they didn't see me run behind them and slide into the driver's seat. A few of the vile mass saw me and turned, but thankfully, I was out of their reach as they lacked the intelligence necessary to operate the door handles.

I watched them for a moment. Tried to find any trace of the humanity behind their eyes. I don't know, I wanted to connect with them in some meaningful way. Maybe I was trying to make myself feel better about what happened. Perhaps, the scientist in me was looking for a way to carve through the madness and come up with a reason behind all of this. Perhaps an easier solution to the problem.

In that moment, I realized, it was all just to make myself feel better.

I lurched the car forward far enough to dislodge my new fans clamoring at the window and lowered the window just long enough to pull the Luger out and offer the only penance I could at the time. I put a single bullet in the young woman's head. It would spare her the fate of becoming a zombie like the rest of them.

After her body settled in the small fountain of water, I hit the accelerator and aimed the vehicle toward Berlin. Stopping to close the gate risked suicide as the mongrel hoard followed the car with surprising speed.

Yet, I still had a chance to make it to Berlin and warn Der Führer.

I hit the throttle and held it to the floor, eking out every last bit of speed the car could muster. The drive wasn't a long one, but there were several checkpoints I needed to go through and each one would slow me down a little on my trek to Gestapo headquarters, which was where I could find out where Hitler was at any given moment. More importantly, it would allow me the opportunity to send a message to him personally.

Gestapo headquarters was located on Niederkirchnerstraße. South of the Brandenburg Tor. Under normal circumstances, it was a little less than an hour drive, but I figured it would take at least an additional thirty minutes to make it through the different gates and checkpoints.

Interviewer: Sounds like it should have been easy sailing from then on out.

Dr. Schmitz: You don't understand how Germany under the Third Reich worked. Everything was checked and rechecked. No one was allowed to simply move from one place to another without clear reason. Remember, this was wartime and the allies had already started bombing parts of Germany with relative impunity. Although people on the streets continued with their lives like Germany was on the cusp of victory thanks to the Goebbels and the propaganda machine. Little did they know the Allied army was the least of their troubles.

The back of my mind never stopped calculating more and more permutations of what was happening to reach reasonable and testable conclusions of possible outcomes. I had already seen how fast the contagion spread, not only from the small building where I was working, but taking over the whole airbase. It spread like an uncontrollable wildfire with no observable end in sight.

That told me the exponential spread of the contagion was reliable overall. There was little stopping it once it reached a critical mass of about two hundred victims, and I knew, from my firsthand observations, we had far surpassed that number already.

Yes, getting to Gestapo headquarters may be the answer, but another grimmer reality clawed its way through my psyche.

If I was even delayed at the checkpoint by ten minutes, naturally there would be no point in getting into the heart of Berlin. Soon I saw the first checkpoint that I—

Interviewer: Sorry, Doctor, but your math skills are better than mine. What do you mean by there was no point?

You see, at the rate of exponential transmission, Berlin would be consumed in a few hours. Think of it this way: If you could shake two people's hands, then each of them could go out and shake two other people's hands, and then that continued. How long do you think it would take for everyone in a city to receive a handshake?

Likely only hours. Now imagine that handshake was a virus that turned the recipient instantly into a blood-thirsty killer who attacked everything in its path, infecting many with a violent fervor. Even a ten-minute delay would have allowed the contagion to catch up and likely overtake my efforts.

No, I glanced at my watch to keep track of the time. Doubtless, I would see it all in the rear-view mirror. Not to say that I wanted to, of course. But at this point, increasingly irrational images continued to assail my mind of a tidal wave of undead German soldiers threatening to overtake me at any moment.

The checkpoint was only a few miles from the Luftwaffe base, and from what I could tell, these zombies could move very fast indeed when driven by the desire for flesh. So even a few miles were still too close for my comfort.

Soldiers guarding the checkpoint waved at me to indicate I needed to slow down. I did as directed, after allowing my fear to momentarily overtake me. All I could do was comply and hope this wasn't going to take long.

During those days, each of the check points had three separate stations. The first was to check your identification card and your operator's license, the next checked your regional papers, and the final was an inspection of the car itself. In those days, there was a good amount of paranoia in Berlin, and they ratcheted down security to ensure saboteurs couldn't enter the city.

The first checkpoint was always the easiest, but I worried about the final inspection the most. As a high-level Nazi scientist, I had papers that would allow me to travel around the Reich almost as I pleased, with the exception of active battlefields. However, I would never be able to reconcile the issue that this was not my car.

The next station, as I imagined, went off without too many problems. My papers elicited a young private to come to attention and then issue a salute with a snappy, "Hiel Hitler." While I was not a military officer, my station in the Ministry of Science and Technology afforded me similar military courtesies with the troops.

At the next station, I met a captain who quickly checked my license and papers again. A hawkish looking thing, he appeared to be too skinny to be a real military officer. However, he certainly had the dour formality of someone who took their menial job running a security checkpoint far too seriously.

With a snap of his heels, he handed me back my papers and ordered me to open the trunk and hood of the car. This was not unusual in situations like this.

I continued to check my rearview mirror on occasion to look for a horde of undead which, by my calculations, were well on their way toward the checkpoint by now. In my mind, I imagined them, bite by bite, surging closer and closer to our location. The contagion spreading. I still had no idea if the bite was the thing that infected the next victim or if it was it simply a matter of close contact.

Further study would be required. But to do that, the first thing I had to do was produce the antidote and the only laboratory I knew of that could accomplish that was currently at my old office and there was no chance I could make my way back there. Berlin was my only hope.

The captain continued his inspection, which felt took several lifetimes. I glanced at my watch and saw that nine minutes had passed since I got to the security check point. If the zombies were headed this way, there was little we could do other than pray for the best outcome.

I was pulled out of my own ruminations over the situation by the slamming of the engine compartment. Moments later, the captain came to me and motioned for me to follow him. I protested, hoping that my station in the Nazi party would carry me through, but he was insistent.

Joining him, he brought me to the front of the car and said, "Herr Doctor, can you explain this?"

I looked down into the storage area and saw that whoever owned this car had apparently been smuggling supplies. My mouth fell open as there were loaves of bread, cheese, and cured meats. I glanced again at the registration of the car and saw the name Sergeant Fischer.

Although I did not know who Sergeant Fischer was, I did know that it was not unusual for visiting officers to bring enough for a small party. Apparently, the car I had taken was designated to carry the food for the gathering surely to have been planned for later on that night.

My mind began to reformulate a plan.

"My good Captain," I replied, "as you know doubt realize, this is not my car. I do not own a car and I needed to borrow one for a quick trip to meet with the Reich minister."

"Herr Doctor, I have no reason to doubt what you are saying. However, I also have no reason to accept what you are saying. I am sorry, but you will have to come with me. For the moment, I am placing you under arrest for violating the rationing order."

As you can see, I was in quite a bit of trouble at this point. I could not argue his logic as it was unassailable. I had no reliable explanation as to why those things were in the car in the first place.

I said, "I applaud your attention to your job, but I hardly think a few supplies stashed in a car that I borrowed are of any consequence in the face of a meeting with Reich's Minister Rust und Der Führer. As you can imagine, I am in a hurry and a delay on your part would be ill advised."

I saw something in his eyes at that moment. His view darted from the food in the car back to me and then back again. And idea crossed my mind. "Tell you what, if you would like to help yourself to some of these items, you may. I'll tell the supply sergeant to take it out of my food rations. You are doing a great job. I can also let Der Führer know when I see him that this checkpoint is the model of party efficiency."

The captain was salivating at the proposition. Some meat, cheese, and bread were almost impossible to find in Berlin during those days, as most of the food was reserved for the frontline soldiers who still had barely enough to fill their bellies. Those assigned to jobs in Berlin were asked to continually tighten their belts for soldiers who needed calories. And as for the supply sergeant, he was likely making his way to this very checkpoint for a meal of a different sort.

I checked my watch to emphasize the need to be on my way, but also to check how long I had been delayed at the checkpoint. The inquiries had me now stopped at the checkpoint a full twelve minutes. By my calculations, it was well past the time I knew I could linger there. And yet, there I was.

The captain started saying something when he was interrupted by a haunting hum coming from the forest in the direction of the airbase. He motioned for me to wait a moment and moved toward the sound, listening to it.

The haunting buzz coming from the forest could best be described as like a noise from a radio not tuned to the station properly. Although clear, it was a low noise that grew in volume by the moment. I stood next to the captain and focused on the source of the noise.

It grew louder until it was almost deafening. I remember being very puzzled by the noise. It reminded me a little of the low hum of a tank as it rolled by. And yet, part of me instinctively knew what it was. Time had run out.

I turned to the captain, who was now completely frozen with the noises we were being inundated with from the forest. I knew I needed to get him out of his stupor and to take some sort of action before it was too late for any of us.

"Captain. Snap out of it. I don't have time to explain why or how, but you have to listen to me. Your men need to move to their defensive positions. Do it now before it is too late."

Out on the tree line it became quickly apparent that my words were spoken at least three minutes too late. The green and loam colors of the wood line morphed into a sea of grey and brown uniformed zombies who pushed their way out of the forest and onto the road, field, and anywhere else they could walk. The highest concentration followed the road I had previously driven. Even if we had a hundred men and unlimited ammunition, there would be no stopping them now.

"Captain, no, listen to me. You need to tell your men to run. Get in cars and drive. It's too late." A quick assessment of the numbers of the creatures told me all I needed. There were more than I could count. I suppose a conservative estimate would be somewhere in the neighborhood of a thousand.

This checkpoint had twenty junior soldiers manning it. Not to mention the probability that maybe half their weapons were loaded, knowing most of the ammunition was sent to the front.

"To your stations!" The captain yelled. The men, sadly, obeyed. He had sentenced his men to join the ranks of the undead.

I tried again, pleading with him to order his men to run, but he refused to listen to me. The captain was fixated on the wall in front of them. His countenance took on that of someone resigned to his fate and unwilling to simply die alone.

Seeing the situation lost, I closed the lid to the trunk, regained the driver's seat, and hit the gas pedal. I left the wood barrier stopping cars from progressing in shards behind me. I needed to get out of there as the forward leading edge of the creatures had a mere 100 meters to cross before they would overtake the checkpoint.

Behind me, I heard orders being given and then an eruption of gunfire. Moments later, the shooting stopped. In the rearview mirror, I could see the horrible truth. The tall captain was now ambling along with the rest of the pack, headed straight toward Berlin.

My resolve failed me for a moment. At the rate of spread, there was little else I could do to stop something so large. Even if I had all the time in the world. And yet, I still had to do something.

Gestapo headquarters was likely not a wise choice as once I was in Berlin it would be next to impossible to get out. Even if I had the time in Berlin, I knew I would not be able to synthesize enough of the antigen before the entire city would be taken over. I knew I needed someplace else to work on the formula.

Interviewer: But you said the laboratory was the only place where you could do the work you needed to do.

Dr. Schmitz: And that is true. However, that does not mean I could not cobble something together and make it work. I, of all the scientists in Germany, could accomplish this task. And then the answer came to me: Spandau.

Interviewer: Do you mean Citadel Spandau? The place the Russians took control of at the end of the war?

Dr. Schmitz: The very same. You see, during those days, we were using Spandau to make the more common nerve agents. Inside, they would have everything I needed. And since the ingredients for the antidote were fairly commonplace, they would have ample supplies on hand.

So, I headed to West Berlin. Spandau, as you know, sits just outside of the city on the Havel river. Based on my calculations, I should have enough time to work out the production plans. A few Gestapo officers were posted to the facility and would have access to communications back in Berlin. At the very least, I could get Der Führer into his bunker and out of harm's way. Perhaps they could organize some sort of response that would keep people safe for the time being. At the very least, minimize the spread.

For the next forty-five minutes, I drove like I had never driven before. I avoided my earlier mistake and drove around the checkpoints by taking alleys I knew would get me to my destination. I can't tell you how relieved I was to see the walls of the citadel rise in front of me.

Spandau is an almost impenetrable fortress. Even today, if a military unit were holed up inside its walls, they would be very difficult to dislodge. When you consider it was constructed in the 16th century, that fact alone should give you pause before undertaking an attack. A small contingent of German soldiers withstood the Soviets for quite a while until it became clear it was all but lost. Even then, the Commander didn't have to surrender. We could have continued until the soldiers were starved to death. And then the ghosts could have just manned the fortress walls.

After showing my identity card to the guard out front, I told him I was on my way to see the chief scientist. He was an old friend of mine by the name of Friedrich. Good man, and a perfectly capable scientist. Sad case really. He and his wife were killed fleeing Germany, as she was a quarter Jew, and that fact came to light during a routine investigation. But that is not a story for our present timeline, is it?

We sat down in his office, and he offered me some coffee and a cigarette, which I graciously accepted. I needed a few of my normal vices to bring my blood pressure back under control and clear my mind. There were so many things swirling around me that I wasn't sure I could get everything out.

In the back of my mind ,that wave of zombies I had spoken about continued to grow. Now, it was a tidal wave. I hated to think how it had grown and what it looked like. That forward edge of the line was likely reaching Berlin proper. What of my uncle living in Spandau? My friend, Eduard, and his wife, Hilda, living on Albertinenstrasse in Zhelendorf? Certainly, they were zombies or dead by now.

It is impossible to divorce yourself from these kinds of thoughts, and yet, that was what I had to do. So, I told Friedrich the entire story. When I was done talking, he picked up the phone and called for the Gestapo man to come into the room. Word must be sent to ensure the survival of Der Führer. That much was certain. On this, everything rested.

As Friedrich went through my notes and we talked about strategy for combatting this bioterror, there was a knock on the door. Friedrich answered and a pudgy little man walked in carrying a small notebook in one hand and his hat in the other. He introduced himself as Felix Metzger.

"Hello Felix, I would like to introduce my friend, Herr Doctor Schmitz. He was working on a secret project down near Ragensdorf and met with some complications that—"

Felix took two steps forward and held up his hand. During those times, if a Gestapo man told you to keep quiet, you did as instructed. While we were certainly important as far as the party was concerned, it would only have taken one hint of noncompliance and you would find yourself rotting in a prison cell. And time was of the essence if Germany was to survive.

"Herr Doctor Schmitz, I am afraid your reputation has preceded you. Although I am quite at a loss why you would come here instead of fleeing to the countryside."

I was astonished by this odd greeting. And, looking back on it now, I should have picked up on the cues. Maybe I was naïve to believe that the scientists were largely divorced from the political nonsense that had overtaken Germany at the time, but in the moment, that didn't occur to me.

Interviewer: But, Doctor, you were a Nazi, too.

Dr. Schmitz: Ja, true. However, so was everyone who wanted to work. If you were a scientist and expected to be allowed to continue in your pursuits of investigation into life's questions, you had to do it. Sure, you could point out that I was working on weapons of war. But I worked in a lab before the war, looking at reanimation. A field of scientific pursuit that has been around since the early 1700s. It was not new. How far is it really to find a way to kill and reanimate a corpse for a short period of time to serve a singular purpose? As it turns out, not that hard. It is shutting them off that proved far more difficult.

But that is what got me into trouble then, isn't it? You see, Felix, as it turns out, was not there to simply meet me. No. At some point, someone reported that I was fleeing Germany with secret documents, and I was to be arrested on sight.

Friedrich protested. "You do not understand. This man is a scientist, and he is here to help us. He would never turn his back on Der Führer. Listen to me, Felix, you must listen to me."

However, Gestapo men were notoriously stubborn. Felix was no different. He pushed his way past Friedrich and grabbed me by the arm. There was little I could do. I was a man of letters, not a street thug. Felix was so much stronger than I was that offering resistance was of little use.

Friedrich continued to yell after him, but that course of action was not going to get us anywhere. I was now officially a prisoner of the Reich. Worse yet, they refused to listen to my protestations about Der Führer being in danger. I was set to sit in a prison cell until one of them came to their senses.

For the next day, I sat in a cell on the lower level of Spandau. My cell, meant only to be temporary, faced the interior of the courtyard. A guard watched over me. Rather unpleasant looking fellow who I would learn was a very predictable sort. He walked back and forth in front of the cell every thirty minutes, allowing me to track time. It was all I had to keep my mind occupied.

Every time he did, I tried to convince him to let me speak with Friedrich. I must have worn him down because he agreed to let me talk with him for a few minutes if I promised to stop bothering him while he went about his job.

After a while, Friedrich was escorted to my cell. Mind you, I was less concerned about myself than I was the papers I had brought with me. They were crucial to the work I was doing. They contained everything we would need to make the antidote in large enough quantities to counteract what I was convinced was now an overwhelming mob of undead filled with blood lust.

"My friend, I'm sorry you got into this," I remember Friedrich saying to me.

"Friedrich, don't concern yourself with my welfare. It's my notes I am worried about. Do you have them?"

"No, they were taken by the Gestapo. For now, I believe they are locked up in the commandant's office. But I must ask you, when do you think we will be overrun? If what you say is true, this is growing exponentially now."

I was glad my old friend understood the issue. However, I could no longer risk him. "I cannot be certain. You can do nothing here if they are locked up. Take your family and head north. Get out of the city for a few days until I can work this out. Leave a note where you will be and ask that my papers be sent to you. When I make it out of here, I will head north to join you in Peenemünde and we can set up a lab there to work on the antidote."

The unpleasant looking guard returned and motioned that our time had come to an end, but I had accomplished all I had set out to do. For now, all I could do was wait and rest in the knowledge that my friend would help me find a cure for what was quickly becoming the undoing of the Reich itself.

For the next day, there was little I could do except pace the floor of my cell, count the half hours by the coming and going of my guard, and watch the comings and goings of Citadel Spandau. That evening, I was awoken from a nap on my very uncomfortable bunk.

"Herr Doctor." I heard the voice of my own personal prison guard say. "You are to be released and taken to the Commander's office immediately. The keys jingling in his hands felt like salvation, but I worried how much time had been lost and how far things had progressed while they figured they had thrown in a prison cell the only man capable of sorting the whole thing out.

Standing in front of the Commandant's desk, I rendered a proper Nazi salute, which you understand, I almost never did as a scientist. However, under the circumstances, I needed to continue to play nice and gain cooperation.

"Hiel Hitler," the Commandant returned the salute. "I am very curious about your work, Doctor. What were you doing when the outbreak occurred?"

I told him the story, as I have told you. Abbreviated, of course, I didn't have time to really worry about the niceties at that point. Unlike Friedrich, he would not have understood the science.

If I wanted to bring this scourge of my own creation to a halt, I needed to get to Peenemünde immediately. I told him. "I must bring my papers there and meet up with my colleagues if there is any chance of us stopping this thing." And then a terrifying thought, well terrifying to me at the time, rose to my consciousness. "And Der Führer? Please tell me he was alerted in time."

"Yes, yes, Der Führer is secure. Once they realized something was wrong, they pulled him into the bunker and sealed it. For the moment, the Fatherland is still in good hands. But I fear for what might happen."

The Commandant, a man whom I had never met, stood from his massive desk and walked calmly to the window. He stood there, staring out into the world like he was lost in thought over a far less trivial matter.

There was something in his demeanor that troubled me greatly. I'm not even sure I have the right words in English or German to tell you really what it was. I guess in German, we would call it *die Seele*, or the soul, in English. I'm not sure that is actually right, either. No, his countenance. There was something wrong with the way he was carrying himself at the moment.

Interviewer: His countenance?

Dr. Schmitz: Yes, you know. Like a man who is laughing at a funeral or someone who is crying at a child's birthday party. It felt out of place. His reaction was completely wrong. Something had happened that caused Der Führer himself to have to go to his bunker for protection, but here he was, playing it all off as if he were taking a report about a traffic ticket.

I finally had to break his silence. "Herr Commandant, I do not wish to seem rude, but time is of the essence. I must make it to Peenemünde to meet my colleague.

So, if I can have my papers, a car and driver, and a few supplies to bring with me, I need to get started."

"Herr Doctor, do you know how I gained this position?"

I was shocked. How would you feel if you were talking to someone, and you explained the most important thing that had to be done at the moment, and all they did was talk about how they got their position at their job? I had no idea how to respond. "Colonel, with all due respect, I—"

"I was a college student at the time, and I found my way into a brownshirts meeting. I put my time and effort into supporting the cause. Really, I only stayed in good graces with the right people and was able to keep myself off the front by calling in favors I had accumulated along the way.

"A little discretion here, the right act there, and I was able, when the time came, to land myself a job that kept my family safe in Berlin while the rest of Germany went to war. I was a coward, in essence. Ironic that I ran right to the very thing that I was trying to avoid."

I stepped closer to him. Whatever held his attention outside concerned me greatly. Using such fatalistic terms could mean only one thing and I hated to admit it to myself. If he was talking in such terms, he wasn't just talking about himself. He was referring to all of us.

Over his shoulder, I could see the front gate of Citadel Spandau. I joke when I say it looked like they were giving out free bakery goods. A mass of inhumanity writhed and slithered around the small gangway to the castle itself. Dozens of zombies had fallen into the moat and made their way to the other side, scraping and clawing their way in a mindless effort to dig through the stone wall.

I moved away from the window and fell into a chair nearby.

My mind raced with a few thoughts about what was happening and how to get out of there. On the desk lay my satchel and I could see the papers were returned to the inside as the flap was open, so I at least still had those.

I turned my attention back to the Commandant. "Okay, Colonel, we need a plan, and we need one fast. I cannot synthesize enough of the formula from here. There must be a way to—"

"Steglitz, my family lives in Steglitz."

I understood what he was intimating. Steglitz was just north of Rangsdorf, where my experiments went so horribly wrong, but I also wanted to remain focused, so I brushed the comments aside. "Understood, Colonel, but we need to formulate a plan to get me out—"

"An armored car was sent house to house, and they found my family. My children tried to kill the soldiers and my wife was found in four pieces in the living room. The soldiers had to leave the house as there was nothing left to do. A photo of me was still clutched in her hand. They shot my children, Doctor."

I'm not incapable of sympathy, you understand. However, we simply did not have time for a lengthy discussion or to really offer any kind of support. This had to stop now before it got any farther. "I understand and I'm truly sorry, but you must also understand that we have a mission and if we are to succeed, we have no choice but to press on. I must find a way—"

What happened next was inevitable, I suppose. In some small way I felt a twinge of guilt for this man's suffering. Does that make me a monster, I wonder? I had unleashed something on the world that resulted in the death of his entire family, and I only felt a little guilt. Perhaps, I should feel some comfort then in what happened next.

Like he had practiced it a thousand times, he pulled out a Kongsburg Colt pistol from his desk drawer, placed it on his temple and pulled the trigger. The act was so smooth and quick, it was like he was pulling a spoon out of a drawer and sliding it into a cup of coffee to stir in the milk and sugar.

The explosion momentarily deafened me while the gasses from the explosion of the powder filled the room, obscuring my vision. Soldiers, who always stood guard outside the door, ran into the room and the resulting change in pressure forced the smoke to abate quickly. I wish it hadn't.

I had never seen a man who had taken his own life up close before. It is a horrifying thing. Blood, brain, and other matter were splattered all over the desk, walls, windows, and carpets. His body lay in a pile on the floor, the gun still clutched in his right hand.

Can you imagine what a gun does to the human skull? Cracks it open like a coconut opened with a sledgehammer. It is possibly the worst thing I will ever see in my life, and I perform experiments that would make your stomach turn.

The soldiers, looking terrified, looked up at me and then down at the body of their fallen Commander. They could have been no more than sixteen years old, and I could tell they had never seen a dead body before. During that time, we had already started pressing kids into service where the threat of armed conflict was particularly low.

A lieutenant of the reserve corps ran through the door and stopped short when he saw the body. He looked from the fresh corpse to me.

I yelled at him. "Lieutenant, I need you to snap out of it. Who is the next most ranking person here at

Spandau?" At the time, scientists were always in charge of Spandau, as the Colonel was. But under him were a cadre of scientists who worked on various formulations.

"Herr Doctor, that would be you."

A silence fell over the place as I pleadingly looked at the faces of the men in the room whose lives I was now responsible for. By a quirk of fate, I was in command. Responsibility I most certainly did not want.

I shook myself from what was suddenly a quagmire of disbelief threatening to pull me under. "You can't possibly be serious."

The lieutenant came to attention and the two young soldiers did the same. "Sir, what are your orders?"

My mind raced at the question. A thousand decisions were possible and likely had to be made, but I could not shake myself from the idea that I must get out of there and to a place where I could do my work. The situation, as it seemed at the moment, was not only dire, but completely out of hand. I needed a miracle.

"Sir, your orders?" The Lieutenant did the only thing he could think of. It was now his turn to shake me from my stupor and while he looked like he feared a reprisal, he did it anyway. It was the very thing I needed to jostle my overtaxed mind into action.

"Send for the senior most military officer on the compound. I need to speak with them immediately. You two privates, remove this body. Take it out into the yard and bury it. I will use the office next to this one for now until this can be cleaned up."

I shouted out orders like a man possessed. A military machine will not work without someone at its head and most of my charges were either young and scared or unfit for combat. I felt like another man for the next hour. I needed order if we were to ever make it out of this mess.

Interviewer: Just out of curiosity, what kind of orders did you give out?

Dr. Schmitz: I did what I had to do. Posted guards on the walls to keep an eye on the zombies. Should any of the undead souls appear to be making any headway to getting inside of Spandau, the soldiers were to shoot them immediately. I also ordered a complete inventory of emergency rations on the site. I had a feeling these soldiers would be there for a while.

I also ordered a search for any vehicle I could use to make my escape. Every room, garage, tent, or anything looking like a structure was being used for the war effort, and most lived in the area so they walked to work. Therefore, there was only one vehicle on site. It was an old, armored car we called a KFZ 13. I'm not even sure you can find them anymore. Even then, they were only found in training units and reserve military formations.

It ran, but only barely. The machine gun had been removed and used for an emplacement near the entrance of the citadel in case anyone breached its formidable wooden doors. I ordered the vehicle readied and for a mechanic to take a close look at it to make it was roadworthy as possible.

In the meantime, an old Reichswehr officer, a somewhat rotund Major with greying hair and sagging face, entered the office I was, for the briefest of moments, calling my headquarters.

I asked if he was the senior most military officer at the compound. He indicated that he was indeed. Then I asked him to carry out the orders and assume the role of temporary Commander of this facility in my absence and he indicated with a nod that he would.

The general countenance of this man indicated he was not only fearful for his own life, but there was something else, too. I don't believe in souls or any other such nonsense, but in that moment, I saw inside him.

This was a veteran of the first world war. A man who had lain in trenches filled with a mixture of blood, mud, mustard gas, and suffering. No doubt that if I asked to look at his feet there would be a few toes missing. At night, he likely drank himself to sleep rather than relive those memories in his nightmares.

Motivations are funny things. With the right motivation, even the most lackluster of a man could be compelled to extraordinary deeds. I needed to tread lightly with this broken man.

I asked him to sit, and I looked directly at him, so there was no mistaking what I was not asking him to do. "Major, I feel that you have had your fill of bloodshed and tragedy. I'm not asking you to fight a war. What I am asking you to do is take stock of what you have, take care of your men, and do absolutely nothing, save one thing. I need to get out of this citadel and on my way north, as soon as possible. I'm trying to meet my old friend, Dr. Friedrich von Hauptmann. He can help me bring an end to this madness I have no doubt you have seen for yourself. Once I am away, lock those doors and secure them as best you can. Then I want you to make contingency plans to protect as many people as you can for as long as you can. You can't stop what is outside of these gates. But you can keep it from getting in. Am I clear, Major? Can you help me accomplish these goals?"

The Major raised himself from the chair, with some difficulty I might add, which confirmed my suspicions of an unspoken and likely violent history and gave me a snappy salute. "I can do these things, Herr Doctor. However, if you are referring to Dr. Friedrich von Hauptmann from this citadel, he was forced to seek shelter further in the city."

As you can imagine, I was momentarily dumb struck by this news. I was relying on him to help me prepare the solutions, tests, and equipment I would need to carry out the work which would save the Third Reich. "How is that possible?" Although I am a man of science, in that moment, I was worried about my friend. The idea of him roaming the world as an undead truly bothered me.

The major shrugged his shoulders. "He was summoned to Berlin to report on your capture to Gestapo high command and had to flee those creatures out there. Last I heard, he had made it into one of the bunkers and was safe for now."

I shook my head at this news. I was truly glad to hear my friend was okay. But this would make it difficult to carry out my plan in a timely manner. Friedrich knew my methods and understood how I liked to operate. He was an extension of myself.

Peenemünde quickly looked like it was out of my grasp in terms of options. If Berlin had fallen and the high command were sequestered to their bunkers, that meant all of Germany was essentially lost. I needed another idea and fast. Yet, it was the Major who pulled me out of my temporary indecision.

He cleared his throat, getting my attention. "Herr Doctor, I know my men are working on the car for you to give you the best chance of getting out of here and on your way. It is up to you where you want to go after this. I can clear a path to let you get across the drawbridge and to the road. That is far as I can get you with our guns. But you need an idea where you want to go. I can give you all the maps you will need for your journey."

The Major mapped out his plan for clearing the bridge. It included two MG 34 machine guns, a few grenades to thin out the mass before the machine guns went to work. After that, the rest would be on me and my ancient, armored car.

He assured me that snipers would provide covering fire, as well as a few men perched above the gate who were excellent marksmen.

Interviewer: Doctor, there is something that bothers me, though. You were working on a cure to revert these people back to their former selves. Doesn't this constitute murder?

Dr. Schmitz: My good man, I was also working on a biological weapon that indiscriminately turned people into mindless killers. Moral relativity has very little purchase on the battlefield. There is a part of me, I will admit, that felt bad about the loss of lives. Yet, if I did not accomplish my mission, none of that really mattered. So, in essence, they were giving their lives for a greater cause.

I watched the men set up their positions and came to understand that I did not give the Major the credit he deserved. Once in a position of command, he was the model of efficiency. Barking out orders, he had named the Lieutenant who responded when the Colonel shot himself, as his adjutant, who took over the role of ensuring provisions, bedding, and other needs were met for the forces who would now find the Citadel their permanent home.

I found the motor pool sergeant, who ran me through the KFZ 13 armored car. Although it was built on an old civil vehicle chassis and I was familiar with its operations, I did not want to make a mistake that could end my life. Once I was out of those gates, the armed car sheeting would protect me on five sides as the top was open. However, the metal was quite high on either side and that would prove to be a critical feature, as I fought my way out of the city. If the zombies were already at the gates and past, it was likely they had found their way west and east of the citadel. And that idea alone was what spurred my decision making.

You must understand that I was a Nazi out of convenience to my trade. But I was committed to the Fatherland. The problem of the zombies had grown so much in such a short time that I no longer had the luxury of picking sides. The scientist in me understood that I must focus on creating this cure at all costs.

The formula, although it was only supposed to be short acting, seemed to have a transmissibility and a longevity that even I didn't understand. Perhaps it was something about the human will to live at all costs or the body's natural ability to focus on what would keep a body functioning that mattered. I did not know at the time. I'm still not quite sure I understand.

In the early thirties, I attended a lecture on cellular resiliency in London. I had given a talk on work I was doing with altering the mitochondria to allow them to continue past their own limits, using a combination of chemical baths and different salt solutions.

After my lecture was over, I met a man who worked in London, named Dr. Bernard Billingsley. I believe you have met him.

We became fast friends and had it not been for the war, we would still be close. However, history and politics put us on different sides.

Bernard and I worked well together. Although not my first choice, he would understand and could fulfill the role I had set out for Friedrich. But that meant I would have to decide to turn my back on Germany, perhaps forever.

There was a nervousness I felt sitting in the driver's seat of that car while waiting for the moment I was told I could start driving toward the gate. The plan was to have the car moving at a slow speed and the gate personnel would open the gate only when I was close enough to accelerate through the opening with no trouble. The thinking was to ensure the car was moving through the gate and the personnel could close the door behind me.

You asked me earlier if I did not consider what I was doing to be murder.

Think what you want of me, but I did consider such things in that moment. My mother wanted me to become an optometrist like my grandfather. Yet, science and the quest for answers beyond our own understanding were like a drug to me. No matter what I did, I could not quit it. And here I was, ordering the death of a hundred zombies who could be saved with something I could easily aerosolize.

Something I knew I needed an expert for.

Interviewer: You said the process was easy though.

Dr. Schmitz: Ja, easy for two scientists working together in close consort, yes. However, for one man all alone, it would be almost impossible to stay ahead of the needed volumes for large-scale production. This is not something I could do at the lab all by myself.

The time for thinking came to an end as two large explosions sounded the beginning of my flight. I took off the parking brake and started the armored behemoth moving forward. Most certainly, this car was far larger than anything else I had ever driven; they generally do not require scientists to drive tanks.

The eruption of gunfire from the machine guns cutting down the zombies was deafening, even at this far off distance. It would only get worse as the time went by. I fought the urge to think about those weapons of war being turned against the formerly alive German people scratching to get into our outpost.

I glanced down at the speedometer to check my speed. I had attained ten kilometers per hour. That was the approximate speed we agreed I would hold to give the machine guns time to do their work. For some reason, that speed felt incredibly fast and remarkably slow all at the same time. Time, when viewed under stress, is a remarkably relative thing.

In front of me, the two soldiers opened the gates that had stood firm against time and all aggressors. I breathed a sigh of relief, knowing it would stand the test of time against this latest threat. Four soldiers, two on either side of the entrance, stepped forward and fired point blank at a few of the undead the machine guns couldn't get to because of their angles of fire.

Approaching the exit for the citadel, I got my first real look at the carnage the machine guns and the grenades had done. I can assure you that no matter how long the good Lord gives me in this life, I will never forget that scene.

Blood, bone, and limbs were thrown everywhere. Zombies cut in half, and not dead, struggled to still reach the only living things within their view. An arm in the remains of a dress lay floating in the moat outside the walls. Body parts that must have once belonged to children lay in a heap in some bushes, undoubtedly the victims of the grenades dropped to the driveway to clear out the mass of inhumanity.

To my right and left, a few lingering zombies were milling about, as you Americans would say, and they turned to attack me the moment it became clear I was a potential snack.

One such wretched creature, a man who looked like he worked in a butcher shop, made it to the car itself and tried to grab on when I saw his head explode. Pieces of him splattered over the front of the car. A sniper's bullet had done its terrifying work with brutal precision.

On the main road, I slowed momentarily to look back at the gates of the Citadel. I had a strong feeling I would never see that place, or perhaps even Berlin, ever again. I breathed a sigh of relief seeing the doors had been reclosed. At least I had been able to assure those men would be safe for now.

I put in the clutch and drove west out of the city, toward a very uncertain future, toward a goal I was unclear I would ever be able to meet. And I would love to say the hard part about this situation was the science and the biology of what I was needing to do. But it really wasn't.

Science is easy. It follows strict rules that are predictable and testable. I was thinking about the war. For all my degrees, awards, and intelligence, I was at a loss when trying to determine how one human can kill another human without logic or reason behind any of it. The pure and unadulterated killing that took place in war was something outside of my own mindset, and yet that was exactly the issue I faced.

Between me and England lay a minefield of issues, both literally and figuratively. Not only did I need to somehow find my way through the German lines, which were naturally suspicious of any Nazi trying to leave German-controlled territory, but the Allies were not likely to just let me come knocking and asking to speak to an old friend who I did a lecture with a few years ago.

In some ways, dealing with zombies was easier. They were at least predictable. Living humans were not.

Magdeburg, Brunswick, and finally, Hanover, lay in my way before I could enter the Netherlands. About a seven-hour drive until I made it to Amsterdam and then I would have to commandeer a vessel of some kind to make it across the channel. An easy feat a few years ago, but now that distance presented an almost herculean task for me to accomplish.

Stopping for the night would not be possible, as I could not risk the horde of zombies, relatively contained in Berlin, spilling out into the other populated areas.

Interviewer: I'm sorry, Doctor, did you call Berlin contained? That does not sound contained to me.

Forgive me, contained may not be the right word. Perhaps isolated, is a correct word? You see, Berlin, although it is a major city, is also isolated in the sense that around it is farm fields and woodland.

I do not mean to sound unforgiving, but outside of Berlin, the infection rate would drop considerably because there were less people to be infected. I know how that sounds, but it is one thing that was working in my favor at the time.

As I made my way through the streets to eventually make my way into the German countryside, the scene horrified me in ways that it pains me to recall. People were out on the streets begging and pleading with those who had only a little while ago been their loved ones. Only to discover, far too late, that they would fall prey to the lustful desire of the undead mind searching for only blood and brain matter to feast upon.

The zombies closest to the road would lunge out at the car to try and grab ahold. Most of the time, they bounced off the car, but sometimes they would slip under the car and I felt the rear tires putting them out of their misery. Or so I hoped.

The fact they would lunge out at a moving car convinced me the rational person inside the human had been suppressed to the point where they had no regard for their own safety. Preservation of one's own life is a human instinct.

But I digress, since this was not the thing I was worried about at this point in my journey as I drove an armored car through the outskirts of Berlin. It was our own soldiers I was worried about.

And yet, I drove as fast as the car would take me. There was this one time. Wait, you don't want to hear—

Interviewer: No, Doctor, I would like to capture as much of this story, as possible. Future generations of scientists will find this valuable.

Dr. Schmitz: As you wish. At one point I slowed down for what looked like a child in the street. The little mädchen carried what appeared to be a stuffed animal, I thought there was no way it could be one of the undead. I nearly opened the car door to try and save the little one when it turned.

Blood smeared from one side of the little girl's cheeks and the front of its clothing. In its hands was not, as supposed, a stuffed animal, but a real creature. The little zombie had caught a rabbit and it was now consuming the brains of the unfortunate creature. It was truly horrifying but it also was interesting to see that the zombies would, if able, feast on the brains of other living beings.

I stomped on the accelerator and the motorized chunk of metal lurched forward, and I did not hesitate to do what had to be done. The sound of a small head and torso hitting the front of the armor told me I had hit my intended target. I felt the rear wheels of the vehicle rise sharply and then fall back down as the tiny body was incapable of holding up such a large mass as the car. You can imagine, I did not stop to look back.

Do not give me that look; I know what I did. I'm not happy about it. And yet, it may have been the most humane thing I could have done. Ask yourself this question: Would you want your own children to wander the world in search of brains? No, I would not imagine so.

I breathed a little sigh of relief when I passed through the city line of Berlin into Oranienburg and I saw far less of the frenzied death on the streets. I cannot exactly say I felt better, but I did feel a bit like I stood a chance of making it to my destination unscathed.

Farmland replaced large buildings and statues of the Kaizer. Instead of cars, horses pulled wagons along dirt roads. It was comforting to know I was out of the maelstrom that had befallen the city of my ancestors.

And that, you see, is when I knew fate had other plans for me. This was not going to be an easy trip. My KFZ 13, even when fully checked out by the motor sergeant, was still a mechanical object and like all, was prone to breaking.

There was a huge explosion, filling the car's cockpit with smoke in an instant. The smell of burning oil and antifreeze threatened to choke me to the point that I almost ran off the road. I pulled the car to the side and got out to look at what had become of the car.

One of the large pieces of armor that protected the engine compartment had blown completely off. Looking down in the direction I had come, I made out the very end of the piece laying just off the paved surface.

Seeing no other choice, I picked up the satchel with my notes and the Luger and began walking in the direction of my destination. With any luck, I hoped someone would find me and maybe drive me into Magdeburg where I could procure another car.

Only a few kilometers down the road, my prayers were answered. Or so it seemed at the time. A Wehrmacht kübel, driving in the opposite direction, slowed down enough that I could gain their attention.

Thinking about it now, I'm sure I made quite a sight. I was walking along the side of the road in a shirt and tie and a lab coat.

They asked me where I was going, and I told them I was headed into the city. I showed them my credentials and asked them if they could give me a lift. I also indicated that there had been a biological accident in Berlin, and they would be unable to return

CLASSIFIED

to the city at the moment. They were far safer headed into the Magdeburg until Berlin could be made safe again.

One of the men, an officer with Wehrmacht intelligence, motioned for me to get into the car, but said very little. The driver turned the vehicle around and took off down the road in the direction they had just driven.

All seemed well, and I relaxed a little, as I thought we would be well and I could make it out of Germany to my destination. The soldiers didn't ask me anything and I didn't engage in any conversation. Remembering the events of that day now, I should have realized that it was a strange situation and perhaps I should have been a little suspicious.

Another ten kilometers or so, the driver made a sudden turn off the main road and drove through a wooded tree line to a house tucked back on a large farm.

I protested and tried to explain to them that making my way further to Magdeburg was of the utmost importance to the Führer and our cause. I even tried to pull rank on them. But they did not listen and instead got out of the car. I was about to renew my protestations when the large soldier grabbed me by the arm and dragged me out onto the ground.

I was aghast. This was no way to treat a scientist of my rank. How dare they treat me this way? I stood from the ground and took a swing at the nearest soldier, but as I explained, I am a scientist and not a soldier. I missed and the next instant, everything went black.

When I came around, my hands had been tied behind my back. My head felt like it had been split in two and my lab coat was covered in blood. I could only assume it was my own.

My eyes refocused on the world around me, revealing empty walls, empty rooms, and an empty floor. I could tell this was an old farmhouse abandoned in haste. Houseplants and other things, still in their pots, were dried and wilted to the point that death had long since overcome them.

I heard a voice to the side of me murmuring something to another, but I could not quite make out what they were saying. Just like if you were at home and someone was talking in the back yard. I could not help but feel as if they were talking about me. Do you know what it is like to have that happen to you? No matter it was not important.

What is crucial to our story is that one of them entered the house from the back door. And you know, it struck me as funny right at that point that I had not thought to check to see if I could move my hands around. They were tied, I could tell, but how well was something that I could not discern.

Interviewer: Why did that strike you as funny, Doctor?

Dr. Schmitz: The thinking man would have likely considered that they needed to escape the situation as soon as practical. And to do that, the first step in the process would be to get your hands untied.

As I said, someone walked into the room. I could tell it was a man by how he walked. I told him, "You do not know who I am. I am a senior scientist working for Der Führer. I must reach Magdeburg. You are impeding my crucial work for the Reich."

The man, a large man with a baritone voice, leaned in close. He smelled of sausages and sardines. "I know who you are, Doctor. I also know how important you are. Or at least I hope you are as important as you think you are."

I growled at the man, "Untie me now. I demand it."

He only laughed and turned around, walking away from me, ascended the stairs, and then I heard him sit down in a chair with a loud noise. He was not, after all, a small man.

Interviewer: Weren't you scared?"

Dr. Schmitz: Naturally, why wouldn't I be? But in the moment, I was more concerned with the spread of F-12 and how quickly Berlin would cease to be an adequate food source for the monsters of my own creation.

As I mentioned before, I had yet to really test my bindings against any kind of real force. I finally had woken up to this fact and pulled hard against them. Unfortunately, the bindings were the most secure I had ever known. He paid attention in his Hitlerjugend knot-tying classes. I guess you would say here, in America, that he paid attention during Boy Scouts.

Unfortunately for him, the chair I was in was old and not in the best of shape. The wood that I was lashed to cracked under the pressure I exerted against it, and it only took me a few more pulls to break it completely free. While the knots were not yet undone, they were free from the chair and loosened up enough that I could work them a little more. Also, since they never tied my feet, I could now stand.

I quickly, and yet quietly, made my way over to the mantel of the fireplace and used the bricks to work free the ropes until one hand was out.

Moving to the door, I looked out to see where I was and what stood against me. Then I remembered my car had been disabled and was not drivable. Their car was still sitting outside and would suffice. Escape was well within my reach, if it weren't for my missing satchel with my notes, and any means to defend myself. I would need to find those items. Everything rested on the research, or I might as well have just died there.

I noticed one of the bricks was loose, and with a little work, I pulled it free of the mantel. While it was not perfect, it did make a convenient weapon. I did a cursory search of the downstairs area and was unable to procure my belongings. I guessed they may have left my satchel in the car, but if I went to look and it was not there, I would have to flee without them.

There was only one thing I could do. I would need to incapacitate my captors and hope I found my items.

So, I crept up the stairs, and just as I crested the last riser, I heard the voice of the man who had come downstairs earlier. He was talking with someone on a wireless device. For a few moments, I listened to the conversation, hoping to ascertain what this situation was all about.

The gruff man said, "I am willing to provide you the location of the doctor for the equivalent of fifty-thousand American dollars in gold. Do not try and pay me in worthless Marks. Answer me within an hour or you will find his body along the side of the road."

The moment he released the handset, another voice came over the speaker. The agitated voice demanded to know who he was and how dare he insult Der Führer by attempting to blackmail the Gestapo.

Then it hit me. These men were nothing more than highway robbers. Can you imagine? During a time of war, where everyone is expected to pitch in for what would have been an inevitable victory for Germany and the triumph of our way of life?

And these men were attempting to extort money from the Reich. It was unconscionable.

As I would like to pretend that I am a highly involved person, far above most, there are moments when even I have given in to my animal instincts. Emotion, something I normally do not indulge in, took over my actions. I tell you that I cannot even recall the events that followed.

The next moment, I stood there, breathing heavily. Sweat dripped down my back and I could feel the blood soaking through my clothing. The man, no, not a man, this common criminal, lay on the floor. The right side of this head, from the temple to the crown were smashed in a good inch or more.

Not proud of my actions, I am more than happy to have ended this man's life for his crimes. There was no real time to reflect on my choices, as I knew for certain there was at least one more man outside the building I would need to deal with if I were to make my way out of this building alive.

On a nightstand, along with the Luger I had been using, I discovered my satchel with my notes. A quick review of the satchel satisfied me that I had all my papers and they appeared in order. I set the weapon on the table next to the wireless. And switched the radio on.

"This is Dr. Ulf Schmitz. I am in a farmhouse East of Berlin, but not yet to Magdeburg. I do not believe I am far off the highway. I am about to leave by stealing one of the robber's cars. Should I be successful in my escape attempt, I will radio from Magdeburg. Over."

As I listened to the reply from Berlin, which was appreciative, yet not too reassuring, a noise behind me grabbed my attention. Out of my peripheral vision I saw a flash of something coming up the stairs. Instinct took over and I grabbed my Luger from the table.

Instinct is oft better than reason and my blind shot was far better than a more prepared one would ever be. The sergeant who had pulled me from the car, clutched at his chest, blood staining through his uniform and forming a growing red blot. The man stumbled backward, and he fell down the stairs.

For a moment, I listened to the house and ignored a plea from the radio to confirm I was still listening. The sound of an engine starting and driving away sent shivers up my spine, and I suddenly realized the remaining soldier, as I recall there had been three, took the car and succumbed to his own fear.

Interviewer: That was your only means of escape, wasn't it, Doctor?

Dr. Schmitz: Well, we shall get to that.

I returned to the radio and conversed with what turned out to be a Gestapo radioman in Berlin. The situation was worse than I had feared. The entire city was in lockdown as the hordes of zombies created havoc on the streets. Pitched battles among the living and the undead were commonplace, as the average citizen lacked weaponry and had to improvise with anything they could find.

Flights of soldiers, trying to escape, made it into the air only to find that one or more were infected with the bioweapon. Planes full of zombies were now force landing all over Germany, where infected creatures were pouring out the back of the planes and attacking the Luftwaffe personnel or citizens wherever the planes had crash landed.

Then I asked the status of Magdeburg. The news was not good. One of the planes, originally destined for Hanover, was forced to land in a field on the outskirts of town. They had been unable to make further contact with the pilot.

With that, I signed off the radio and in a final act or revenge against my captors, I shot the wireless set so if the remaining criminal decided to circle back around, I would rob him of his ability to communicate.

Grabbing my satchel, the gun, and any ammunition I could find on the dead soldier, I made my way outside. Checking in all directions to ensure there were no zombies, or additional soldiers lingering about, I looked out into the driveway. Indeed, the Kübel was gone.

Behind the building, there were three large barns. The first contained farming equipment common to any farm and of little use in my predicament. The second looked like it had an airplane retrofitted for the application of pesticides and that kind of thing. While I had one course in how to fly a plane at the German military institute, I was not prepared to fly a plane solo, no matter how brilliant a scientist I am.

In the next barn I was lucky. Sitting under a canvas tarpaulin, I discovered a beautiful, practically new, BMW R75 motorcycle. As unfamiliar as I was with flying an airplane, I was as familiar with the operations of a motorcycle, having raced them prior to the war.

Soon, I was on the road again and headed toward Magdeburg. I almost felt normal riding my absconded motorcycle. The open road was just that, devoid of any traffic. I was happy for it, as I needed a break and it looked like I was finally getting one. The city lay ahead of me and beyond that lay Brunswick and Hanover. From there, I would be able to get out of Germany and into Allied hands.

You could say that my outlook was brightening significantly. I even risked a smile at the idea of synthesizing a cure, saving as many as I could, and then writing several more papers on the whole ordeal.

I could even see a Nobel prize for my work in physiology in my future.

Interviewer: Doctor, I hate to sound like a bit of a cynic here, but don't you think it a bit out of touch to daydream about getting recognition for inventing a cure for a plague that you created?

Dr. Schmitz: And why not? I did the work to create it in the first place. There were probably hundreds of hours' worth of research that went into creating the biologic weapon in the first place. So, it would only be natural that the cure would be considered a natural extension of that work. Would it not?

After all, I had already figured out the cure and only needed a laboratory and an assistant who could help me make it happen. Don't I deserve credit where credit is due?

Now, if you are done criticizing my genius, can we continue?

Interviewer: By all means. Please continue, Doctor.

Dr. Schmitz: Well then, I was riding down the road and making very good time of it. The roads in that part of the country are mostly straight and you can see for quite a few kilometers in front of you.

A distance off, I could not tell you how far, smoke filled the sky. Not a fire of a building that I could tell, it looked to be emanating from one of the farm fields.

Another kilometer or two, I can't really remember how far, I made out what was certainly some sort of crash. During that time, there was not a single German alive who did not know what a burning vehicle looked like. It was too commonplace, as the Allies were turning the tide of the air war.

I slowed my approach to get a better look at what happened. The brain is an amazing thing, gentlemen. It can connect dots through space and time and make sense of what is happening instantaneously. A single wing ripped off the fuselage of a Junkers-53 transport told me all I needed to know. That must have been the aircraft the Gestapo man told me about on the radio. The doomed flight of the undead.

Stopping on the roadside, I looked over at the plane. The rear of the fuselage was ripped off, like a can opener had taken to it. My only hope was that the undead were all destroyed in the crash, and that they had not escaped and made their way toward the town. I could only pray that didn't happen. But, I needed to be sure.

Turning the motorbike off the road where a farmer had a small access trail to the fields, I made toward the plane. My hope was that I could confirm they were all silenced by the impact of the crash. I had to be sure, since even as few as one ambling undead wandering the countryside posed a significant threat to us all.

It could also mean that Magdeburg, and maybe other cities throughout Germany, were already infected with the virus and the spread was reaching an unmanageable level.

I kept the bike away from the flames, as the heat from the wreckage was already putting off an unimaginable heat. Even if the zombies had survived, any of them trapped near the wreckage would be boiled in their own juices, as it were.

I walked toward the rear of the plane to get a better view of the inside. At first, it looked like no one was inside, but in a brief gust of wind, I made out a few forms. As none of them were moving, I guessed they were all dead. To the right of the plane, my attention was directed toward a moaning sound.

Luger at the ready, I approached the source of the sound, prepared for just about anything in this new world I was realizing had more in common with nightmares than the dream world the Third Reich was trying to build.

One of my former colleagues was trapped under a piece of the wreckage that had been flung during the crash. Half of his mutilated body was crushed into the ground. In a more whimsical mood, I could guess he was growing out of the farmer's field like summer wheat, but my mood had soured considerably, as you may guess.

There was nothing I could do for the man as he was no longer human. I stood there for a moment and watched the zombie claw and scratch at the ground. It tried to scream at me, but it looked like the lungs of the former Luftwaffe Colonel were collapsed under the weight of the fuselage piece.

Have you ever just stood and looked down upon the summation of your creation, as well as the equation of your own failures? If you ever have the chance to do so, I suggest you don't. I will be forced to live with that reality the rest of my natural life.

At that precise moment, I realized that perhaps I had gone too far. Maybe, there are times when we are capable of doing things, but need to demonstrate the wisdom necessary to refrain from doing it.

Interviewer: Doctor, you of all people understood what was happening better than anyone else. Why should that moment strike you as more important than anything you had witnessed before this one?

Dr. Schmitz: Only God himself can answer that question. Perhaps it was He who was forcing me to look down at that unfortunate man struggling against everything. And I knew what it wanted. Simply to feed. Given the chance, it would feast upon my brains or perhaps infect me to have me join the denizens of the undead roaming the German countryside.

The next moment, I felt the cold steel of the end of the Luger against my temple. The impossible suddenly felt possible in my mind. Ending it all, right there and then, was the only logical thing to do.

All my years of training, time spent analyzing biochemical reactions and studying the effects of human physiology, didn't amount to anything. The weight of the world crashed down upon my shoulders.

Another moment and then sweet relief of oblivion. I said, out loud to only the zombie trapped before me, "May God forgive me for what I have done, or the devil punish me justly for my crimes."

Interviewer: Obviously, Doctor, you did not pull the trigger.

Dr. Schmitz: Fate, the heavens, or who knows what interceded in that moment. A stick snapping on the ground behind me shuttered my resolve. I turned to see the ambling form of an undead soldier making his way across the field toward me.

In the muted sun of the overcast day, I recognized the man. It was the criminal who had taken the car back at the farmhouse. But, not really him, at all. Perhaps it is best to say he deserved it, I don't know, but he'd been infected.

I couldn't take the cowards way out. No, I erased that notion from my head. Although, I have no doubt that if that specific zombie had not made an appearance just when it had, I would not be here to tell my tale.

I had to keep fighting until I drew my last breath of air. I knew it then. God himself required I keep going to try and make amends for what I had done.

I fired one shot into the criminal-turned-zombie's head, sending him reeling backward toward the plowed earth. Then I fired the next shot into the unfortunate man pinned to the ground.

Moving from the plane, back toward the motorcycle, I was stopped in my tracks by four men holding rifles. One of them, a man named Matteus, a Finish man, stepped forward, "Lower your weapon, we have you outnumbered. Are you Herr Doctor Schmitz?"

I lowered my Luger and eyed the man. How did he know my name, what did he want with me? I responded that I was. Another man, Ivan, moved forward and motioned for me to hand over the Luger. "You have nothing to fear from us, Herr Doctor, we are here to help you get to safety."

"You are resistance, then?" I asked.

Ivan nodded. "Well, I suppose we are really just the survivors at this point."

"Forgive me, gentlemen, but for now, I wish to keep my weapon. I am not sure if you have noticed, but the need for a firearm has suddenly become more important than ever." I was unclear on what he meant by survivors. It seemed hasty to surrender my only means of protection.

Ivan nodded toward another man, who nodded his acceptance. I would soon learn his name was Lukas, an American from Ohio.

An hour later, we lifted off in a repurposed German airplane flown by a man. As we made the turn toward England, and I looked down on Magedeburg, I almost reconsidered staying my suicidal hand.

Flames had erupted all over the city. Hordes of undead had taken over and pushed their way into walls of the infected, rolling over the small pockets of resistance. There was no salvation for Magdeburg, or possibly Germany for that matter. And that meant, there would be no salvation for me.

Or so I thought. At least I suppose that is what you are here to find out, isn't it?

Interviewer: Come on now, Doctor. I have no idea what you mean.

Dr. Schmitz: My friend, don't play coy with me. You are at a minimum, trained in the sciences. Perhaps a doctor yourself. I could tell by the look in your eyes that nothing I have said during this interview has surprised or confused you. My feeling is that you were sent in here to find out—

Interviewer: Doctor, come now. I am only here to interview you—

Dr. Schmitz: Am I but a child? You know my work, that my story is accurate. There was no need for you to walk in this door today. I suppose you already have my papers. And yet, you are here. More importantly, I can say that I am not in Nuremburg, dangling from a rope. So, let us put away childish things and speak frankly. What do you really want?

Interviewer: This is Dr. Stephen Kozlowski, COL U.S. Army, concluding the interview of Dr. Ulf Schmitz. Recording ended.

TRANSCRIPT FILED: 23 June 1946

// Dr. Stephen Kozlowski, COL U.S. Army //

///////////////NOTHING FOLLOWS///////////////

September 15, 1953

"Excuse me, Dr. Abrams?"

"Yes, Michelle. Please come in."

"I have those forms ready for your signature, Doctor."

A plump man reclined slightly in his chair and pulled a pen out from the side drawer. "Excellent, let's have them." He briefly glanced at the forms and then signed them, one by one, with the bureaucratic efficiency that comes with having signed thousands of similar forms. "How are things around the base this morning?"

"The usual, sir. You know, at some point, I stop paying attention to what is going on and just go about my day."

"I told you, when it is just you and me, call me Carl. I hate all this military formality." Dr. Abrams frowned at his secretary, who had been faithfully by his side through the last two years. She knew more about him than most people did.

"Yes, sorry about that. Again, I sort of fall into a routine." She sat down in one of his deskside chairs while he finished signing the papers.

"Don't we all. Say, have you been over to Dr. Schmitz's lab this morning?"

"No, Carl, I haven't. Why?" The way she said his name made her look like she was trying it out for the first time and was deciding how it sounded out loud.

"Just wondering. I got a phone call from his lab this morning and it sounded like there was some commotion in the background, but I couldn't be sure. I may pop over there after this. Any plans for the weekend? Barb and I are going to work on the garden."

Michelle, a slim brunette woman in the ubiquitous woolen suit of an executive secretary, shivered and stood from the chair. "Nothing really. I may return some library books. I have my exams next week." She glanced off into the distance and frowned at an unseen thought. "His work creeps me out. The idea of creating zombies to perfect an antidote really scares me."

Carl stood and came around the desk and put a hand on her shoulder. "Believe me, it doesn't freak me out any less. But, if we want to prevent this from happening here, we must let him work." He gave her a smile and then turned to the papers on the desk. "Here you go, all signed and ready for filing."

"I'll do that right away." Something in the distance, outside the large bay window of the office, grabbed her attention. "What is that?"

"What is what?" Carl asked, and they both moved toward the window in unison. In the distance, billowing smoke from behind the tree line gave the distinct impression something had gone wrong on base. "Michelle, what's in that direction?"

"I am pretty sure that's Dr. Schmitz's lab."

Note to the reader: Nazism was a horrific scourge upon the world and left scars that still can be seen and felt on our planet today. At the same time, it needs to be stressed that most Germans are wonderful people and we Americans have more in common with them than we do many other people on this planet. The German military is a steadfast ally to our armed forces worldwide. So, why on Earth would I write this?

Simply stated, the idea for this comes from a videogame I would love to play, but does not yet exist. I always wanted a videogame where you played a NAZI scientist who has to fight their way through zombies, their own troops, and then the Allies, so he can bring a copy of his scientific finding to a British colleague who can help synthesize the antidote. I always thought that would be a heck of a game to play. Guns, explosives, zombies, epic battles you have to cross, tanks, trucks, airplanes, and motorcycles would make this an epic adventure. And yet, I have not seen this videogame.

I wanted a new novella to offer my fans and I knew this was a story I would like to read, so not seeing another like it, I took to my keyboard.

Nazism and extreme nationalistic ideologies are ultimately a threat to freedom. While the main character is a committed Nazi, I wanted to show how flawed his thinking was by the interjection of the interviewer who tries to point out the flaws in his logic, but ultimately is really only there to make sure the story is recorded.

Acknowledgements: First off, I have no one to thank more than my family. My wife and kids for tolerating hearing my crazy stories and off the wall ideas, the time I spend in my room and at shows where I sell my books, and all kinds of other insane things I do. Most of all, Mrs. Nowak, for being my first reader.

I also want to thank the wonderful people of Germany where this book is set. We spent three years living in Germany in Berlin, in Zhelendorf and the places I mention in the book are places I have personally visited. I actually bought a cloak at a sidewalk festival at Spandau and I still wear it.

If you have never been to Germany, I urge you to go. It is a wonderful place, and well worth taking a vacation to see.

I need to thank my editors and publisher for being kind and not telling me I was an idiot too many times. While my hand may be on the tiller of this ship, there are plenty of people behind me, telling me if and when I need to make course corrections.

CLASSIFIED

END

www.ingramcontent.com/pod-product-compliance
Lightning Source LLC
Chambersburg PA
CBHW071945190726
48293CB00004B/1363

9781954214293